Disney Princess

Look and Find Picture Puzzles

Briar Rose sings to her forest friends.

Search the scene to find 10 differences.

66

67

For the solution, turn to page 118.

Look closely to find 10 differences in each pair of pictures! For the solutions to the puzzles, turn to the back of the book.

Illustrated by the Disney Storybook Artists

Published by
Louis Weber, C.E.O., Publications International, Ltd.
7373 North Cicero Avenue, Lincolnwood, Illinois 60712

Ground Floor, 59 Gloucester Place, London W1U 8JJ

Customer Service: 1-800-595-8484 or customer_service@pilbooks.com

www.pilbooks.com

p i kids is a registered trademark of Publications International, Ltd.

Look and Find is a registered trademark of Publications International, Ltd., in the United States and in Canada.

8 7 6 5 4 3 2 1

Manufactured in China.

ISBN-13: 978-1-60553-131-1   ISBN-10: 1-60553-131-6

Look and Find® Picture Puzzles

pi kids® publications international, ltd.

Belle is always reading, even when she takes a walk.

Find 10 differences in Belle's hometown.

For the solution, turn to page 102.

Aladdin spots Princess Jasmine in disguise.

Search the market to find 10 differences.

For the solution, turn to page 102.

Cinderella has many furry and feathered friends.

Look for 10 differences in Cinderella's bedroom.

For the solution, turn to page 103.

Mulan loves to paint pretty pictures.

Find 10 differences around Mulan's bed.

For the solution, turn to page 103.

Prince Phillip visits the newborn Princess Aurora.

Search this royal scene to find 10 differences.

For the solution, turn to page 104.

The evil Queen is busy creating wicked spells.

Look around the Queen's lab for 10 differences.

For the solution, turn to page 104.

Pocahontas sings to her forest friends.

Find 10 differences in this nature scene.

For the solution, turn to page 105.

The mermaids and mermen swim to Triton's palace.

Search this underwater scene to find 10 differences.

For the solution, turn to page 105.

Snow White makes a wish at the wishing well.

Look around the well to find 10 differences.

For the solution, turn to page 106.

Disguised as a prince, Aladdin enters the city.

Find 10 differences in the parade scene.

For the solution, turn to page 106.

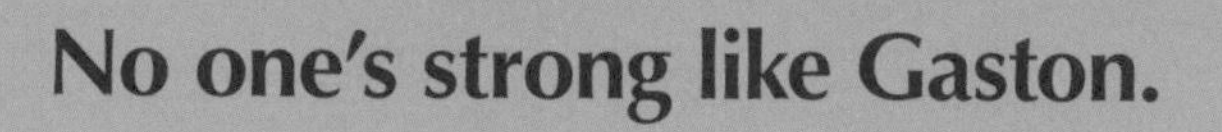

No one's strong like Gaston.

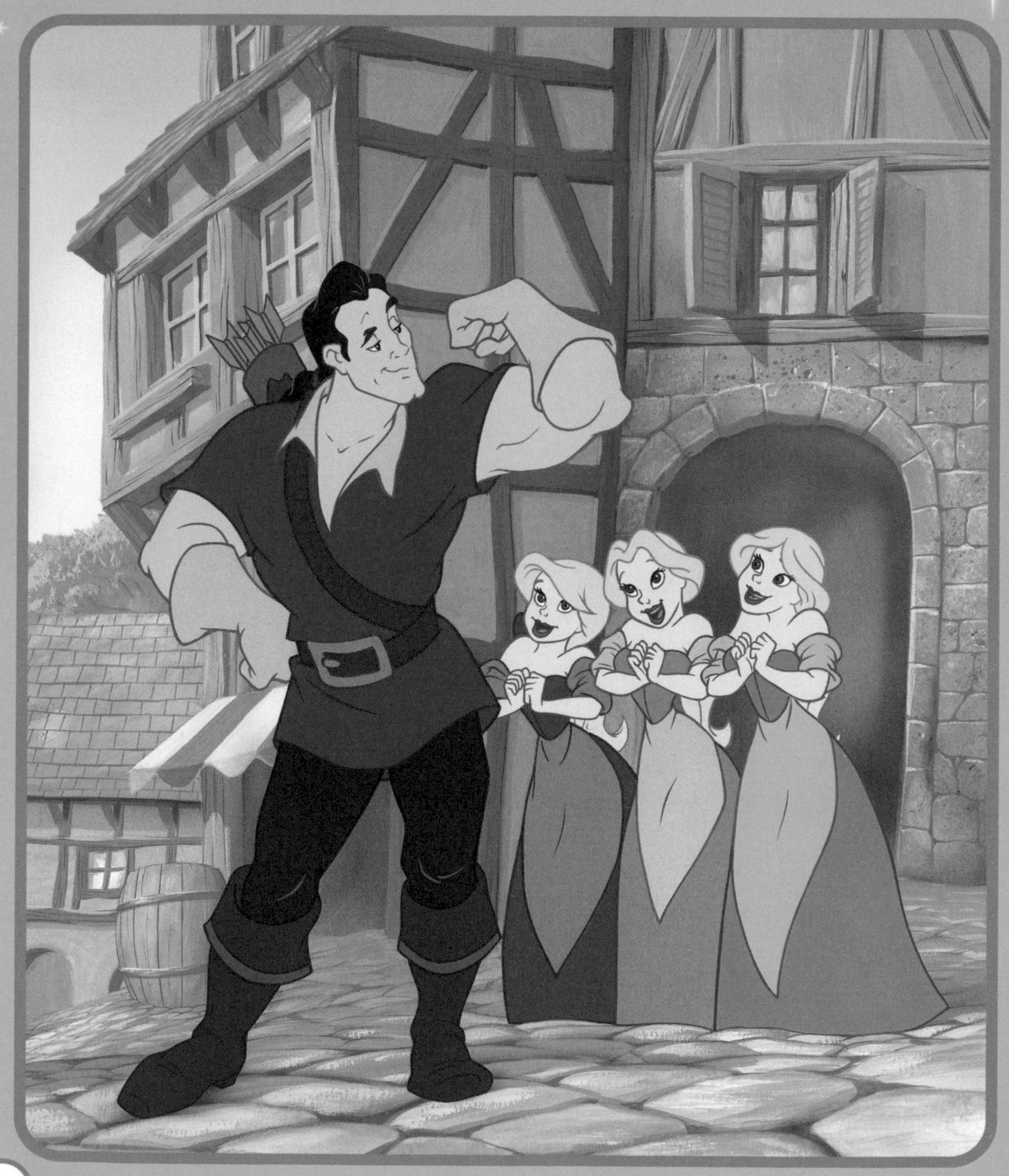

Search Gaston's village to find 10 differences.

For the solution, turn to page 107.

Cinderella and her friends do their chores.

Look around the barnyard for 10 differences.

For the solution, turn to page 107.

Atlantica is all set for Ariel's big concert.

Find 10 differences among the eager audience.

For the solution, turn to page 108.

Belle's father is quite an inventor!

Search the smoky lab for 10 differences.

For the solution, turn to page 108.

The royal subjects celebrate Aurora's birth.

Look around the palace entrance for 10 differences.

For the solution, turn to page 109.

Mulan has made quite a mess!

Find 10 differences in this messy scene.

For the solution, turn to page 109.

Some forest friends keep Snow White company.

Search the forest floor for 10 differences.

For the solution, turn to page 110.

Cinderella daintily pours cups of tea.

Look around the kitchen to find 10 differences.

For the solution, turn to page 110.

Ariel's sisters are shocked to find her missing.

Find 10 differences around Ariel's empty shell.

For the solution, turn to page 111.

Snow White finds a cute little cottage in the woods.

Search around the cottage to find 10 differences.

For the solution, turn to page 111.

Pocahontas meets a handsome man named John Smith.

Look for 10 differences around Pocahontas and John.

For the solution, turn to page 112.

Cinderella is always working very hard.

Find 10 differences as Cinderella climbs the stairs.

For the solution, turn to page 112.

The Genie gives his friends a big hug.

Search for 10 differences in this friendly scene.

For the solution, turn to page 113.

Belle enjoys an enchanted dinner.

Look for 10 differences in the Beast's dining room.

For the solution, turn to page 113.

Snow White tidies up the cluttered cottage.

Find 10 differences around the Dwarfs' house.

For the solution, turn to page 114.

Cinderella admires her pretty dress.

Search the sewing room for 10 differences.

For the solution, turn to page 114.

Ariel loves collecting human treasures.

Look for 10 differences in Ariel's secret spot.

For the solution, turn to page 115.

Prince Phillip meets Briar Rose in the forest.

Search around the stream for 10 differences.

For the solution, turn to page 115.

Each day, the Dwarfs work hard in the mine.

Find 10 differences in the Dwarfs' mine.

For the solution, turn to page 116.

Cinderella's friends make her gown beautiful.

Search for 10 differences in this scene.

For the solution, turn to page 116.

The Beast makes some new friends.

Find 10 differences on and around the Beast.

For the solution, turn to page 117.

At last, Ariel is living life as a human!

Look for 10 differences at the royal dinner table.

For the solution, turn to page 117.

Briar Rose sings to her forest friends.

Search the scene to find 10 differences.

For the solution, turn to page 118.

The Seven Dwarfs march home from work.

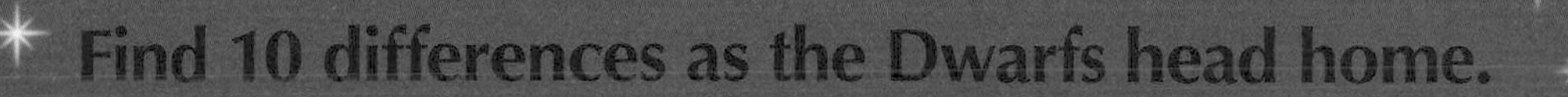

For the solution, turn to page 118.

Aladdin and Abu go for a magic carpet ride.

Look for 10 differences as the friends fly by.

For the solution, turn to page 119.

The Beast and his servants are free from the spell.

Search the scene for 10 differences.

For the solution, turn to page 119.

Cinderella admires her magical coach.

Find 10 differences in this charming scene.

For the solution, turn to page 120.

Ariel and her friends swim to rescue Prince Eric.

Look for 10 differences on the open sea.

For the solution, turn to page 120.

Mulan practices her action moves.

Search for 10 differences as Mulan trains.

For the solution, turn to page 121.

Pocahontas sings of the colors of the wind.

Find 10 differences as Pocahontas sings.

For the solution, turn to page 121.

Fauna blesses baby Aurora with the gift of song.

Look for 10 differences in this magical, musical scene.

For the solution, turn to page 122.

The Dwarfs wait for their sleeping friend to wake up.

Search the somber scene to find 10 differences.

For the solution, turn to page 122.

Aladdin and Jasmine celebrate their wedding!

Find 10 differences at the wedding.

For the solution, turn to page 123.

Belle has such wonderful family and friends!

Look for 10 differences at Belle's home.

For the solution, turn to page 123.

Cinderella begins her happily-ever-after!

Search for 10 differences as the wedding bells ring.

For the solution, turn to page 124.

Ariel and Prince Eric are together at last!

Find 10 differences around the wedding ship.

For the solution, turn to page 124.

Astride her horse, Mulan is a brave hero.

Look for 10 differences on the crowded street.

For the solution, turn to page 125.

John Smith and Pocahontas marvel at nature's beauty.

Search the skies to find 10 differences.

For the solution, turn to page 125.

Princess Aurora has found true love.

Find 10 differences around Aurora and Prince Phillip.

For the solution, turn to page 126.

Snow White rides off with Prince Charming.

Look for 10 differences as Snow White leaves.

For the solution, turn to page 126.

This is the answer key to the Picture Puzzle on pages 2 & 3.

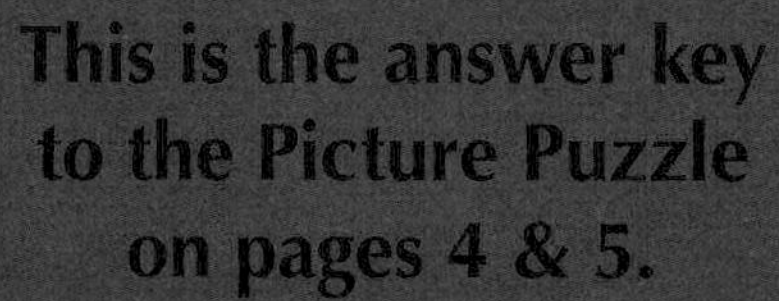

This is the answer key to the Picture Puzzle on pages 4 & 5.

This is the answer key to the Picture Puzzle on pages 6 & 7.

This is the answer key to the Picture Puzzle on pages 8 & 9.

This is the answer key to the Picture Puzzle on pages 10 & 11.

This is the answer key to the Picture Puzzle on pages 12 & 13.

This is the answer key to the Picture Puzzle on pages 14 & 15.

This is the answer key to the Picture Puzzle on pages 16 & 17.

This is the answer key to the Picture Puzzle on pages 18 & 19.

This is the answer key to the Picture Puzzle on pages 20 & 21.

This is the answer key to the Picture Puzzle on pages 22 & 23.

This is the answer key to the Picture Puzzle on pages 24 & 25.

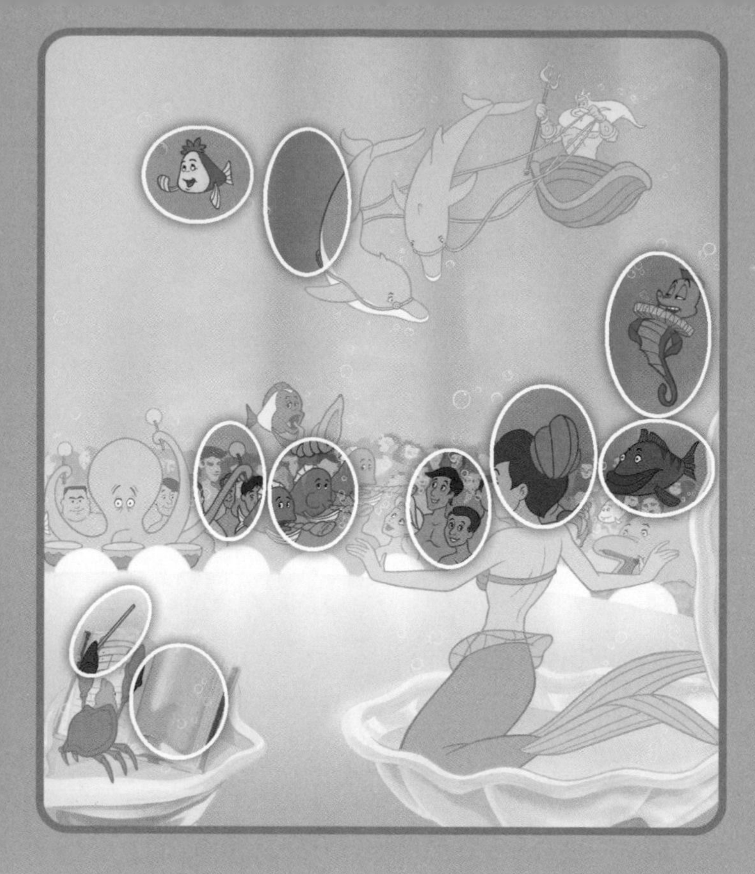

This is the answer key to the Picture Puzzle on pages 26 & 27.

This is the answer key to the Picture Puzzle on pages 28 & 29.

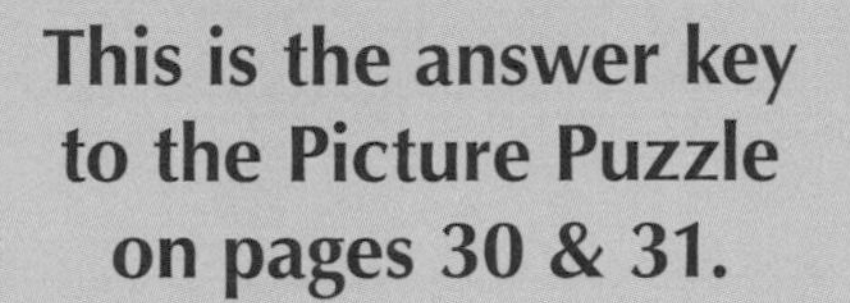

This is the answer key to the Picture Puzzle on pages 30 & 31.

This is the answer key to the Picture Puzzle on pages 32 & 33.

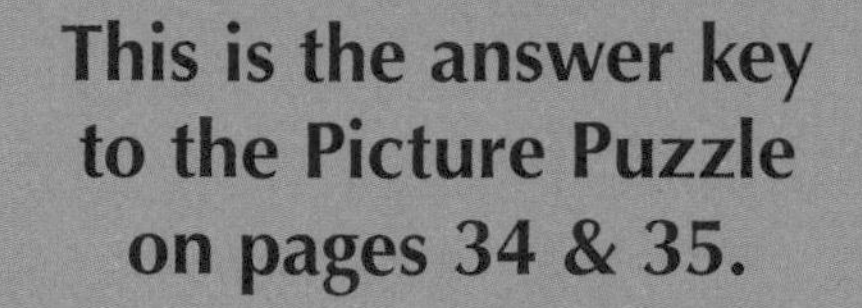

This is the answer key to the Picture Puzzle on pages 34 & 35.

This is the answer key to the Picture Puzzle on pages 36 & 37.

This is the answer key to the Picture Puzzle on pages 38 & 39.

This is the answer key to the Picture Puzzle on pages 40 & 41.

This is the answer key to the Picture Puzzle on pages 42 & 43.

This is the answer key to the Picture Puzzle on pages 44 & 45.

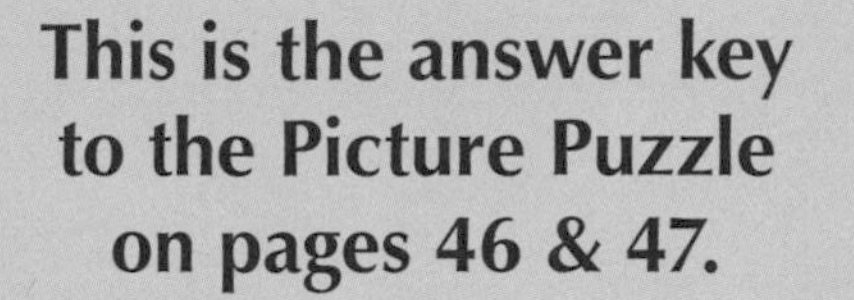

This is the answer key to the Picture Puzzle on pages 46 & 47.

This is the answer key to the Picture Puzzle on pages 48 & 49.

This is the answer key to the Picture Puzzle on pages 50 & 51.

This is the answer key to the Picture Puzzle on pages 52 & 53.

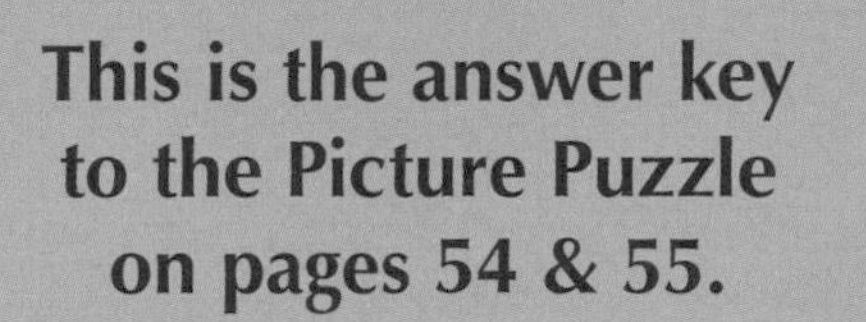

This is the answer key to the Picture Puzzle on pages 54 & 55.

This is the answer key to the Picture Puzzle on pages 56 & 57.

This is the answer key to the Picture Puzzle on pages 58 & 59.

This is the answer key to the Picture Puzzle on pages 60 & 61.

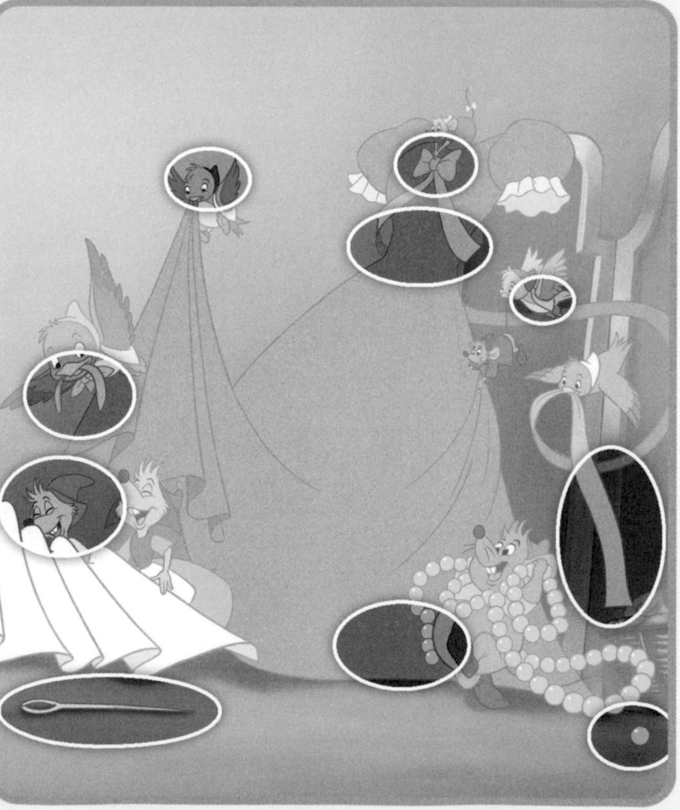

This is the answer key to the Picture Puzzle on pages 62 & 63.

This is the answer key to the Picture Puzzle on pages 64 & 65.

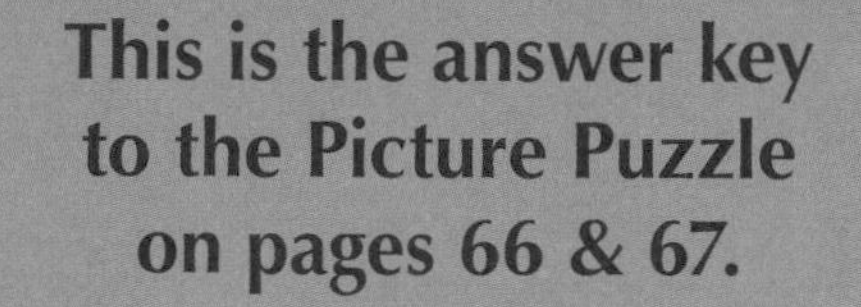

This is the answer key to the Picture Puzzle on pages 66 & 67.

This is the answer key to the Picture Puzzle on pages 68 & 69.

This is the answer key to the Picture Puzzle on pages 70 & 71.

This is the answer key to the Picture Puzzle on pages 72 & 73.

This is the answer key to the Picture Puzzle on pages 74 & 75.

This is the answer key to the Picture Puzzle on pages 76 & 77.

This is the answer key
to the Picture Puzzle
on pages 78 & 79.

This is the answer key
to the Picture Puzzle
on pages 80 & 81.

This is the answer key to the Picture Puzzle on pages 82 & 83.

This is the answer key to the Picture Puzzle on pages 84 & 85.

This is the answer key to the Picture Puzzle on pages 86 & 87.

This is the answer key to the Picture Puzzle on pages 88 & 89.

This is the answer key to the Picture Puzzle on pages 90 & 91.

This is the answer key to the Picture Puzzle on pages 92 & 93.

This is the answer key to the Picture Puzzle on pages 94 & 95.

This is the answer key to the Picture Puzzle on pages 96 & 97.

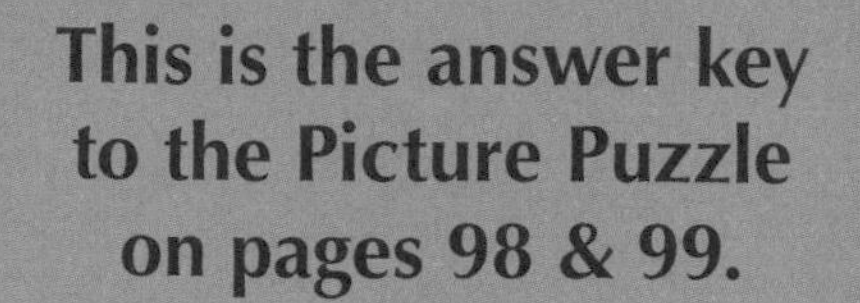

This is the answer key to the Picture Puzzle on pages 98 & 99.

This is the answer key to the Picture Puzzle on pages 100 & 101.